Dear Parents,

Welcome to the Scholastic Reader series. We have taken over 90 years of experience with teachers, parents, and children and put it into a program that is designed to match your child's interests and skills.

Level 1—Short sentences and stories made up of words kids can sound out using their phonics skills and words that are important to remember.

Level 2—Longer sentences and stories with words kids need to know and new "big" words that they will want to know.

Level 3—From sentences to paragraphs to longer stories, these books have large "chunks" of texts and are made up of a rich vocabulary.

Level 4—First chapter books with more words and fewer pictures.

It is important that children learn to read well enough to succeed in school and beyond. Here are ideas for reading this book with your child:

- Look at the book together. Encourage your child to read the title and make a prediction about the story.
- Read the book together. Encourage your child to sound out words when appropriate. When your child struggles, you can help by providing the word.
- Encourage your child to retell the story. This is a great way to check for comprehension.
- Have your child take the fluency test on the last page to check progress.

Scholastic Readers are designed to support your child's efforts to learn how to read at every age and every stage. Enjoy helping your child learn to read and love to read.

> **—Francie Alexander**
> Chief Education Officer
> Scholastic Education

To Betsy Lewin
—G. M.

To Seraphina Dilcher
—B. L.

Text copyright © 1995 by Grace Maccarone.
Illustrations copyright © 1995 by Betsy Lewin.
Activities copyright © 2003 Scholastic Inc.

All rights reserved. Published by Scholastic Inc.
SCHOLASTIC, CARTWHEEL BOOKS, FIRST-GRADE FRIENDS, and associated logos are trademarks and/or registered trademarks of Scholastic Inc.

Library of Congress Cataloging-in-Publication Data is available.

ISBN 0-590-26264-5

10 9 8   06 07
Printed in the U.S.A.   23
First printing, November 1995

THE
CLASSROOM PET

by Grace Maccarone
Illustrated by Betsy Lewin

Scholastic Reader — Level 1

Cartwheel
·B·O·O·K·S·®

SCHOLASTIC INC.
New York Toronto London Auckland Sydney
Mexico City New Delhi Hong Kong Buenos Aires

It's the day
before Christmas...
It's almost three.
The class is sitting quietly
to hear who gets
the classroom pets.

The snake goes home with Kim.

The rabbit goes with Dan.

The ant farm goes with Max.

The hamster goes with Jan.

Sam gets the crab.
Her name is Star.

Oops! Star falls down
in Mommy's car.

Sam gives Star water.
Sam gives Star bread.

Sam says good night
and goes to bed.

Sam wakes up
to something great.
Star is eating
from her plate.

In the kitchen,
Sam lets Star crawl
across the floor,
along the wall.

Sam turns around
to get a pear.
When Sam turns back,
Star is *not* there!

Where is Star?
Where did she go?
Sam looks high.

Sam looks low —

under the bed,

under a chair,

with the toys.

No! Not in there!

Sam wants to cry.
Where could Star be?
Now Sam sees
the Christmas tree!

Then Sam takes back
the classroom pet.
And this is a story
that Sam won't forget.